WOLF ACADEMY
Jonathan Allen

SO YOU WANT TO BE A
BIG BAD WOLF?

ORCHARD BOOKS

Once upon a time two wolves came upon a poor orphan wolf wandering in the forest. They had no cubs of their own, so they decided to adopt him.

The months went by and the little wolf
seemed happy in his new home with his new
family, although he didn't get involved in
rough and tumble play like his wolf cub friends.

And he was a bit more friendly towards other animals than a wolf really should be.

He told it to them straight.

And his parents did just that.

At The Wolf Academy, the new pupils sat in silence. The Head Instructor gave them their introductory talk. He told them about the Six Steps to becoming a true Big Bad Wolf.

This was followed by a video called, 'Who's Afraid? So You Want to Become a Big Bad Wolf?'

Before they began their training, the young wolves had to stand up and introduce themselves.

Our orphan wolf didn't get off to a good start.

Then it was time to learn about Step One – Leering and Lurking. The Instructor lined up his pupils in front of a large painting of the forest and gave them their instructions.

They leered and lurked for all they were worth.

The Instructor was impressed, but not by Phillip.
He couldn't leer and lurk to save his life.

Maybe Phillip would be better at Step Two – Snarling. The Instructor prodded Phillip with his paw and gave him a nasty smile.

Phillip tried his best, but he wasn't very good at snarling either. The other wolves sniggered, but not for long. . .

The Instructor narrowed his eyes
and drew a deep breath.

The young wolves couldn't disagree.

The next day it was time to learn about Step Three – What Little Pigs Use to Build their Houses.

The Instructor gave a Huffing and Puffing demonstration.

But there was more to being a Big Bad Wolf than Huffing and Puffing, or Leering and Lurking, or Snarling. There was Attitude. You had to *want* to be big and bad. This was Step Four.

Phillip just didn't have the right attitude.

It was almost dark as the young wolves crouched at the edge of the forest to learn about Step Five – Howling. The Instructor waved his baton and a chorus of blood chilling howls echoed through the trees.

He was pleased until he listened closely to Phillip. Phillip's howl wasn't blood chilling, and it certainly didn't have that effect on the Instructor – it made *his* blood boil!

With a snarl, the Instructor broke his baton over his knee and threw it into the trees. Quick as a flash, Phillip bounded after it and came back with the two halves in his mouth, wagging his tail.

Big Bad Wolves have to know how to disguise themselves as sheep. They do, it's in all the stories, and this was the Sixth, and final, Step. The young wolves were just putting on their sheep's clothing, when Phillip started acting very strangely.

He flung off his sheep disguise and began
darting around their legs, nipping at their
ankles and growling.

The Instructor watched in amazement, then suddenly it struck him. Now he knew what was bothering him about Phillip. No *wonder* he wasn't very good at being a Big Bad Wolf!

He took Phillip to see the Head Instructor who was very understanding. He told Phillip he knew about another school in the next valley, which he would find much more to his liking. Phillip could be sure of a place there because. . .

. . . in case you haven't guessed, Phillip wasn't a wolf at all, especially not a Big Bad one. He was a sheepdog! A poor lost sheepdog who had been mistaken for an orphan wolf while wandering in the woods.

And Phillip loved his new school. So from being a not very good Big Bad Wolf, he soon became the star pupil at The Sheepdog Academy of Excellence.

And what's more, he always kept in touch with the kind wolves who had brought him up.